For Euan, who demanded worse rabbits
Simon Puttock

For Lilli & Bum
Judith Drews

First American edition published in 2008
by Boxer Books Limited.

Distributed in the United States and Canada by
Sterling Publishing Co., Inc.
387 Park Avenue South, New York, NY 10016-8810

First published in Great Britain in 2008
by Boxer Books Limited.
www.boxerbooks.com

ISBN-13: 978-1-905417-86-5
ISBN-10: 1-905417-86-1

1 3 5 7 9 10 8 6 4 2

Printed in China

All of our papers are sourced from managed forests and renewable resources.

MR. MAC'S BAD RABBITS

Written by
Simon Puttock

Illustrated by
Judith Drews

Boxer Books

MR. MAC lived all alone,

and this made him rather sad.

Then one day he invited some rabbits to stay,

but, I am sorry to have to say,

those rabbits turned out to be BAD!

They chewed with their mouths open,
talked with their mouths full,
picked their noses, and
stuck out their tongues.

They were messy and unhelpful, foul-tempered coots

who never took baths and smelled like old boots

. . . and said VERY RUDE WORDS
(unrepeatable ones).

And was Mr. Mac at all bothered?

No. He just smiled and said, "Rabbits will be rabbits,

and these rabbits are my friends!"

But that was not the worst of it.

WHY, those bad rabbits made fun of Lucy Lapin's brand new cherry blossom hat.

("Balderdash!" said Mr. Mac. "It's none of MY affair.")

They teased the tail and pulled the whiskers off Harvey O'Hare's cat. ("Fiddlesticks!" said Mr. Mac. "I really couldn't care.")

They **PIDDLED** all over
Betty Bun's **EXPENSIVE**
oriental mat.

(And Mr. Mac said,
''Monkeys! Monkeys-in-the-zoo!
Rabbits will be rabbits,
and **THAT IS THAT!''**)

But one day, Mr. Mac went away,
and what did those bad rabbits do?

They nibbled the toes
off his stripey socks,
put all his favorite books
through the dryer,
trampled his purple
hollyhocks,

and set the kitchen stove on fire,
scribbled all over
the downstairs hall,
stole the batteries
out of the TV remote,
tore the wallpaper off the walls,

turned his bathtub into a boat,
AND did something unmentionable
behind the sofa!

When Mr. Mac came back,

did he smile and say, "Who cares?" No, he did not.

Mr. Mac was FURIOUS, Mr. Mac was

HOPPING MAD. He was absolutely LIVID.

He cried, "My rabbits are JUST TOO BAD!"

"Ha," said Betty Bun, and, "Monkeys! Monkeys-in-the-zoo! RABBITS will be rabbits, and that is that, pooh-pooh!"

"Ha," said Harvey O'Hare, and, "Fiddlesticks to you! Rabbits will be rabbits, and what do you expect ME to do?"

"Ha," said Lucy Lapin, "and lots of balderdash too! The terrible truth of the matter is simple . . . your rabbits are just like YOU!"

WELL! Mr. Mac was taken aback.

He'd never thought of it like THAT!

"Something has got to be done about this,"

he cried in **great alarm.**

"My rabbits must learn
to have much better HABITS,
before they do any more harm!"

So Mr. Mac set his bad rabbits to
LEARNING:
table manners,

and flower arranging,

being tidy and

being polite,

how to tie shoelaces, how **not** to make faces,

how to tell right from left, and wrong from right.

How to choose curtains and
how to coil rope,
and things you can do with a
washcloth and soap.
And that, you might think,
was the end of the matter–

those rabbits were good now, those rabbits were fine, but those rabbits enjoyed getting better and better. Those rabbits decided they wanted to SHINE.

They took lessons in dancing,
and how to say "please,"
and "thank you," and how to
plant carrots and peas.

They learned how to cook, and read
interesting books,

and not give the neighbors

unsettling looks,

and how to weave carpets,

and decorate hats,

and **how to be gentle**

and loving to cats.

In fact, soon those rabbits
had PERFECT habits,
but Mr. Mac . . . well, he was just as bad as ever,
and **that** was not good enough!
So those rabbits packed their bags
and wrote a simple goodbye note:

"Dear Mr. Mac, we are leaving you,
and if you want to know why, the terrible truth of the
matter is simple: WE are now FAR TOO GOOD for you.
. . . So, dear Mr. Mac, Goodbye!"

And Mr. Mac said sadly,

"Monkeys! Monkeys-in-the-zoo!

Here I am, all alone again–

oh, what am I going to do?"

BUT WAIT!
What's this?

A scratching and a tapping at the door?

Look! Mr. Mac has found some mice!

And, oh! Those mice are . . . NOT VERY NICE!

But Mr. Mac says,

"WONDERFUL!

The merrier, the more!"